Journey To Inner Healing

Journey To Inner Healing

Abidah Chiera

Journey To Inner Healing
Copyright © 2020 by Abidah Chiera

Library of Congress Control Number: *2020923648*
ISBN-13:   *Paperback:*   *978-1-64749-281-6*

General Fction

All rights reserved. No part of this publication may be reproduced, distributed, or transmitted in any form or by any means, including photocopying, recording, or other electronic or mechanical methods, without the prior written permission of the publisher or author, except in the case of brief quotations embodied in critical reviews and certain other noncommercial uses permitted by copyright law.

Although every precaution has been taken to verify the accuracy of the information contained herein, the author and publisher assume no responsibility for any errors or omissions. No liability is assumed for damages that may result from the use of information contained within.

Printed in the United States of America

GoToPublish LLC
1-888-337-1724
www.gotopublish.com
info@gotopublish.com

Contents

About vii
Acknowledgments ix
Chapter 1 Start of an Unknown Journey 1
Chapter 2 Reviving My Body 11
Chapter 3 A New Hope.. 21
Chapter 4 Pain and Struggle 31
Chapter 5 Reality of Emotional Distress................................ 39
Chapter 6 A Personal Reflection Thought............................. 45
Chapter 7 A Glimpse of Hope... 53
Chapter 8 Reviving Myself 59
Chapter 9 Believing in Myself... 67
Chapter 10 Triumphant.. 73

About

The story highlights the hardships and sufferings of a woman who is not only emotionally challenged but is also hindered in a drastic manner when it came to her physicality. The book is about Abidah Chiera, a woman who not only fought against the odds, but also triumphed in the test that we call life.

Acknowledgments

I gratefully and sincerely acknowledge my grandfather Rufus for his immeasurable input in my life during my early childhood—that all things are possible if you keep trying. I also acknowledge my father Chrispus who believed in me no matter what.

Special thanks to my dear mother Lydia, a strong woman of faith, who taught me to believe in all possibilities. She taught me from my childhood to believe in all acts of hope and miracles. My mother is treasured dearly by all those who know her. Thank you, Mother, for your undying love, care, support, and ceaseless prayers.

Thanks to my treasured sister Eunice who left her home to care for me during the acute phase.

Thanks to my sister Elizabeth and her husband for their relentless service.

Expressions of sincere gratitude to my cousin Jacqueline who helped my sister take care of me.

Thanks to Ben.

Thank you to my family-friends Jim and Eva. I could not have survived without your uplifting weekly visits. Thank you for your provisions.

Thank you to my friend Maina. You are great in your own way.

Special thanks to Charles and Mary. You are an amazing couple that no words in the English language can be used to describe. Thank you for the laughter and hope you brought to my death bed. You held my hands up when I could not. You fed me when I couldn't eat. You are still with me as I write this book. You are my true friends. I am thankful for you.

Tasha and Mr. Brown, thank for your undying courage to save my life. You were the first respondents. You are brave in all that you do.

I cannot forget my healing team members, those who held me in prayers every day, my great faith and prayer team from Baltimore, Maryland, and my faithful friends and prayer team, Nancy, Catherine, Beatrice, and all the women of Dallas and Fort Worth, Texas, who supported me during this challenging journey.

My friend Lucy came to see me every day, without fail. She brought joy and positivity in my otherwise bad situation. My dear friend, you were there to alleviate all the pain and bad news with the power of prayer. I held you in my heart as I wrote this book.

Thank you to Mr. Arthur and his wife for inviting me to their house for a prayer meeting that changed my life forever.

I cannot forget to mention the prayers of faith by Open Door Church in Burleson, Texas, and friends from UK and all over the world. May God bless you.

Thank you to the volunteers of Meals on Wheels, Tarrant County, who brought me a hot meal when I was alone. I looked forward to seeing your smiling face every day. You never fail to deliver, even in bad weather. I urge everyone to support this volunteer group of Tarrant County - Fort Worth. They genuinely care.

And last but not least, thank you, physicians, nurses, and social workers who made my life easy. Special thanks to Celia and Irma for all that you've done. I am entirely grateful.

Chapter 1
Start of an Unknown Journey

I remember it like it was just yesterday. A life experience this traumatizing was very hard to forget. My name is Ciera, and this is my story.

    It all started when I woke up with an odd feeling one sunny morning. I couldn't put my finger on what it was, but I knew I was going back to my hometown, and my clinical rotation was finished. I got ready and put my scrubs on just like every other day. Work was the same, which got me thinking about how routine my life had become. I had lately been convincing myself that I was perfectly happy. But I had never admitted that, deep down, I sometimes craved companionship. I believed God had a plan, and the situation I was in and everything that I was feeling then was all a part of his plan.

    I picked up dinner on my way home from work and decided to pick up a few hats for my mom; she loves to dress up. I came home and went straight to the bathroom to take a nice long bath, unwind a bit from the hectic weeks I'd been working long hours at the hospital. What people don't know is that nurses never had it easy.

I ran a bath and decided to gather my stuff in the meantime. Even the sound of water didn't make it any less quiet, so I put on some gospel music. I am a Christian woman, and there was always something about gospel music that always fascinated me. Hundreds of people gathering to sing praise for the Lord, all with the biggest smiles on their faces, clapping their hands with such energy and happiness; it all just gave me a very positive vibe every time. I'd even say it was my pick-me-up.

I got so lost singing and clapping as I packed that I didn't notice the water from the bathtub had started to overflow, so I ran to the tub and turned the faucet off. I felt like I was finally in a good mood, compared with the state of mind I'd been in all day. So I got into the bathtub (still listening to the music from my room) and relaxed. As I said, I was feeling better, and I was even smiling now for no reason at all. I felt a twitch in my right leg, but I ignored it and continued conditioning my hair and listening to music.

Suddenly, I felt my body slide further down into the water, and it felt like I was numb. I had no control of my body. I tried moving my legs, but I couldn't. I couldn't even feel them, let alone move them. I couldn't even push myself up enough to get out of the water. I flailed my arms and shoulders in a desperate attempt to do something, anything at all that'd save me from drowning, drowning in my own bathtub, in my own house. I couldn't believe what was happening. I knew I could feel my body giving up on me. That's all I could feel. I couldn't feel my toes, my feet, my legs, my knees, my hips, and my waist.

My heart sank. I thought to myself, maybe this was it; perhaps it was time to go. Could *this* be God's plan? I felt tired and weak, I didn't think I could fight, so I let my body loose, and I stopped struggling. I gave in. My head was submerged in water, and just when I was seconds away from blacking out, I heard the music fading. Somehow I made out the words from the fading music that said, "I'm still in the fight, help me!" and it hit me. God's plan couldn't possibly be for me to give up. God didn't make me a quitter. I called out for help, and I asked God to save me, even though I thought it was too late, and I was already gone.

I opened my eyes and decided to fight. I reached for the faucet to pull myself up with one hand, hoping that it didn't break, and I used the other hand to unplug the bathtub to drain out all the water. As I lifted my head out of the water, I gasped for air. I never thought I'd lay in a tub having just fought death with every bit of strength in me. I didn't know what to think; I didn't know what to do. I screamed my lungs out and cried really loud because I was still in shock. My mind couldn't process whatever had just happened.

I still couldn't feel my legs or anything else from the waist down. I used every bit of my upper-body strength and dragged myself out of the bathtub and crawled across the bathroom floor into my bedroom, pulled out my phone, and dialed 911 to call the paramedics for help. I asked them to let themselves in through the front door, and I fainted. Even though I was unconscious, I still remember everything. I remember lying there on my bedroom carpet dripping wet, soaked in soapy water and despair.

When the paramedics arrived, they wrapped a blanket around me and carried me into the ambulance and rushed me to the hospital. All I remembered was the nurses clearing the hospital corridor as they made way for the stretcher with me on it. The doctors ordered all sorts of tests, scans, and medicines. Luckily, all of which I could understand since I'm a nurse. I heard the doctors speaking and learned that I had suffered a severe paralysis with no known cause. Listening to so many frightening words being said about me all in one sentence scared me to death. I'd always empathized with patients and their families, but I never knew it was this bad. I was all alone and scared of what would happen next.

I remembered the nurses asking around for my emergency contact, but I was unable to give out any information because of my inability to speak. That was the extent of my weakness. I never thought something this physically and psychologically painful would happen to me. That's the last thing I can recall before I completely blacked out. Even though it seemed like the hard part was over, it had just begun. From that point forward, everything was a test—a test of my capabilities, my strength, my persistence, my resilience, and most of all, my faith.

I opened my eyes to an unfamiliar environment. A tall man dressed in blue scrubs looked at me and asked me what my name was.

"Ciera," I said.

"Do you know where you are?" he asked.

"No," I replied

"Do you remember what happened, Ciera?" he asked.

I didn't entirely remember what had happened. But all I knew was that I felt weak. I felt weak, and I couldn't move. I didn't feel anything, and I couldn't move. I slightly lifted my head and looked at my feet. The man in scrubs tapped my feet with a flashlight and looked at me.

"Can you feel that?"

"No," I said as I smiled with a heavy heart.

"My name is Dr. Macrod, and I'd like to talk to you about your health, Ciera," he said.

When I looked at him, he began to explain to me that I had suffered a severe spinal cord injury and that half of my body was paralyzed (just like I heard the doctors and nurses say).

"We're still going to run some tests to make sure everything is okay and to find out what caused it, but for now, please stay as relaxed as you can," he told me.

I smiled at the kind doctor, still feeling too weak to speak. The nurse walked in with a tray of medicines and attempted to engage me in conversation to make me feel better.

"Is there anyone we can call?" she asked.

I shook my head from side to side, and she smiled and told me that it was going to be okay. I wasn't entirely sure if everything really was going to be okay, but I didn't know what to expect or think anymore because I was still in shock about how I survived what I survived all alone. One thing was for sure: I was beginning to see life in a whole new dimension. As I ventured deep into thoughts, I realized I was actually getting weaker and weaker as each moment passed. I was losing control of my body, my own body. I wasn't functioning the way I should've been, and I was struggling to keep my composure.

Days later, I woke up slightly aware of my surroundings but still severely sick. Dr. Macrod came to me and talked about the results of some diagnostics procedures. I told him I was a nurse, and I can understand the terms he was using.

"You're a nurse, right?"

I nodded.

"Your new tests came back, and we're not sure what caused the spinal cord injury. I can't specifically point out why or how you lost your body function from the waist down, but it was what caused the paralysis. We're looking into it, and we'll let you know as soon as we have an update," he told me.

I realized this was the start of a long sick journey full of struggles. Judging by the doctor's expressions, I knew it was severe and that they didn't tell me the severity of the situation to not worry me more than I already was.

I wasn't sure why I wanted to go back home, but I knew that wasn't going to happen anytime soon. My condition was deteriorating instead of improving. And before I knew it, days transitioned into weeks, and weeks transitioned into months. I kept the faith and spent months in the hospital; each day I hoped and prayed a little harder for God to restore my health and well-being. The next morning the nurse came in and saw me looking gloomier than usual.

"I know it's hard. But you still need to push through everything," she said.

"I understand," I replied, trying to keep it together.

"You're going to need all sorts of therapy."

"What sorts?" I asked.

"Occupational therapy and physical therapy while we continue to treat your spinal cord for inflammation with steroids," she said.

I realized I had to start accepting that I will be wheelchair-bound with no telling whether I will ever regain my mobility again.

Three months later, the doctors planned to discharge me to a long-term care facility. Since I was still suffering from paralysis from the waist down and still very unstable, not many long-term care facilities were interested in taking me in because my health insurance had expired, and I was an insured citizen who did not qualify for any government assistance. Regardless of the bad situation, I still felt hopeful. I knew that it wasn't time to worry about anything else but my health.

I felt a gush of positivity flow in me. My mind was at ease, and even though I feared the reality I was facing, I couldn't give up on being healthy again. I was faced with several challenges, from not working to no longer being able to care for myself. I still convinced myself that I was ready to conquer just about anything and everything. I was surrounded by what I called a healing team. This team was composed of people of faith, prayerful people, and they offered me a shoulder to lean on during my healing process. So I went back home; nothing was the same. I was hoping things would go back to the way they used to be. I hoped and prayed to fall right back into my routine, but it was a dream so far away.

The thought started to settle on my mind, that I was no longer able to take care of myself, that I could no longer bathe myself, feed myself, or turn myself in bed. I was fully aware of my condition by now, which only made it worse for me. The journey of facing challenges daily outside the hospital was real as ever. I became emotionally weak and terrified of the bathtub but still didn't have a choice but be in it since I was being groomed. Everything came back to me, and I could feel my heart race when I remembered how helpless I was lying in that bathtub, fighting for my life. I can still hear the sirens blaring in the back of my head.

I imagined what would've been if somehow I hadn't gathered the courage to fight. I thought to myself that nobody could've survived what I had survived. With no desire to live again, I prided myself for the fight in me and felt blessed to be alive. Speaking of which, I thought day and night about how I unplugged the bathtub and saved myself from drowning to my death. How could someone in such a chaotic, life-threatening situation possibly think that fast? That was when I realized that God had saved me for a purpose. I was destined for great things in life.

I had always been a good Christian, but this incident had restored my faith entirely. I believed that there was no possible explanation for how I was alive except that God saved me.

God says, *"In the day of my distress I will call on You, for You will answer me,"* Psalm 86:7.

This was then my most cherished verse. It was the closest to my heart. I knew that the second the thought of dying crossed my mind, if I called out to God for a brief moment, somehow he would answer. And he did!

I had always thought of myself as an average woman who had done enough to qualify as a good human being in the eyes of society, but I never felt that I had pleased God enough for him to give me a new life. I was filled with gratitude and joy.

As mornings passed by with no progress, losing control of my body even more, I still had hope of one day getting out of bed on my own. I wasn't well enough to travel back home to Maryland. I felt as if my life needed purpose since I was looking at life in a whole new light. I knew either I gave up the struggle by being bound in bed forever or fight through this and rise above it all so that when I'd hopefully be better, I'd be able to encourage another person, and they'd get to learn from my experience. I chose to use my brain since it's still intact. I longed to go to church to enjoy the worship and positive, uplifting aura. I wanted to stand up one more time from my wheelchair, and most of all, I longed to be healthy again. Most things seemed to fade away in value and importance as I went through this process of healing.

For the first time in eight months, my sister Elizabeth, with the help of others, took me to church; the service was still in progress when we had arrived. We went inside and made our way to the handicapped area. What happened next shook me! I didn't believe what was happening was true. I heard the choir singing the same song I'd heard when I had almost drowned to my death. I felt as if they were all looking at me and smiling as they sang.

I started singing along with tears streaming down my face. I had never felt so alive. I felt as if I'd been revived. My sister Elizabeth loves to sing, so she joined in the chorus. It was a wonderful feeling, everyone sang together, and I felt something that I hadn't felt in a long time—hope.

The sermon began, and I couldn't believe how close I felt to God.

"God loves all his people. He does not discriminate. God always helps us in difficult times."

"Amen!" the crowd all yelled together.

> *The Lord says, have I not commanded you?*
> *Be strong and courageous. Do not be afraid;*
> *do not be discouraged; for the Lord,*
> *your God will be with you wherever you go.*
> *—Joshua 1:9*

"*God* has instilled immense courage and strength in all his people. Which is why he has commanded us not to give up hope. No matter how hard things get, God's people always fight and push through."

"Amen!" the crowd yelled again.

I realized then, at that very instance, that God was speaking to me. He appreciated me for not giving up when I had reason to give up the most. I realized that I was among his chosen ones. I didn't give up on myself, and God didn't give up on me. I felt blessed, and I was gleaming with hope.

"And God indeed doesn't ever let go of his people. For no matter how far away they may go from him, they're still his people, and God doesn't forget that. God tests his people and then lets them see for themselves how much they mean to him," said the pastor.

"Amen!" yelled the crowd again as they all got up and joined the choir and began to clap their hands and sing along. The pastor then pointed right at me and asked me to join everyone. And so I did. I sang my heart out, I cried, I clapped my hands, and I looked up and smiled. I thanked God for blessing me as he did.

It's like there was happiness in the air all around as I went up, and everyone welcomed me by embracing me and introducing themselves. It's like they all knew I was coming. Nobody knew who I was, but everyone made me feel so special. Again, it's like God was making me feel happy and helping me recover from the most traumatic experience I'd ever had.

I felt amazing. I felt like my body was fully responsive, even though it wasn't. I felt like I was in the best state of mind I'd ever been. I felt overpowered and overjoyed. Even though I was still feeling physically weak, it was like I was given a new life, one that was full of hope, strength, and joy. I knew I had looked forward to this moment my entire life; it was finally here.

Chapter 2
Reviving My Body

I ended up in the hospital with lesser hope and strength than I've ever had before. I didn't know what to say, I didn't know what to think, I didn't know what to do, and I most certainly didn't know how to feel. I was stripped of my fundamental human right—the right to live. Was my life even worth anything anymore? I didn't have anyone by my side; I felt alone and hopeless. I knew for a fact that in my entire life, I had never done anything so wrong to deserve an experience like the one I got. All I had was myself, and after everything, I couldn't even say that I had myself.

I know a person can't control everything, but one thing that I had hoped to control was my body. It sounds bizarre because nobody states the obvious, but that wasn't the case with me. I had no control over my body, unfortunately. I felt weak and helpless, and even though I didn't know how or if I was going to make it through, something still felt positive inside me. Not that I really paid a lot of attention to it because I was clearly going through hell, and I didn't possibly have the time or strength to think about anything else except my health and whether or not I'd ever be okay again.

The doctors kept ordering all sorts of tests and scans, but none of them caught what was wrong with me, not even the slightest clue. The most they could do was keep running tests and ruling out all the possibilities. But I knew if it kept going on that way, there weren't enough resources on the planet to help rule out every possible disease. And even if we tried, it wouldn't make even a bit of sense because I had drowned in debts, and I couldn't even afford to be alive, so I knew very well I couldn't be spending money that I didn't even have to begin with. It all made no sense to me.

The hospital gave me physical therapy, which honestly made no sense at all since nothing in my body from the waist down was functioning. It was just money wasted, and I knew nothing good was going to come from it. Not that I had started to become a cynic, but being a nurse, I had enough medical knowledge to know that physical therapy had no business before a proper diagnosis.

As far as my body concerned, I was absolutely helpless. Nothing from the waist down was functioning, which, obviously, meant I couldn't do anything at all physically. My digestive system was failing, as well as my liver and my kidneys. Almost all my vital organs were giving up on me. I still couldn't figure out why I was even still alive and kicking (well, not exactly). But it made no sense to me, just like everything else. Clearly, my state of mind wasn't the strongest. What made everything so much worse was that even though my body was practically useless when it came to functioning, I still had a fully functioning and responsive brain.

Why was that worse? Because it made everything so much more real than I needed it to be. If my brain wasn't doing so good, I wouldn't remember whatever was happening to me. I really wish that would've been the case. I couldn't stand the pain and agony; nobody would cherish a life like this. Was I supposed to? I had so many questions running through my mind, but nothing that made me feel any different from the miserable state I was in. These four walls seemed to be getting tighter and tighter; I felt suffocated.

When I asked the doctor when I could leave, he told me he certainly didn't have an answer for that question, but the primary issue was whether or not I'd be going home at all. I stared in complete shock; my heart was beating faster than it already was. I was scared to ask him, what now? But I did it anyway, and what happened next was just as I'd expected, maybe even worse. The doctor looked at me with sorry eyes and offered me a few wise words of encouragement before suggesting end-of-life care with a comforting hand on my shoulder.

End of life? Is that what it had to come to, my life was ending? I was well aware of the dire condition my body was in and what awful circumstances it was enduing, but I didn't think the solution was just to give up and let my lousy luck win. Trials are afflicted on us for a reason—to make us stronger. God didn't just create us, bless us, and test us for us to give up. He likes his people fighting for what they believe in, and I wanted to fight! Regardless of how difficult it seemed right now, I knew I just had to.

One would think that I had enough to deal with already, and as hard as it was finding the strength to get through what I was going through, God felt like I still had some power in me, I guess, because along came another trial. My insurance company informed me that my insurance had relapsed. I had little to no money to get past such a difficult situation. Literally, the only thing that could've made it worse was something of this sort happening, and so it did. The way I see it,

God has created his people, and he knows what they're capable of. He knows what they can endure. So even though I felt like I had reached my breaking point, I still believed that God wouldn't ever afflict trials on me more than my capacity, which clearly meant that I'd get through this too. He just wanted to see the fight in me and make me realize how strong my faith is.

So I began to discuss my financial options with the doctors. I needed to find a way out of everything one at a time, so I decided to start with finding an alternative to my program. When I inquired about my options, I realized I was stuck. I didn't qualify for a lot of the government supplemental programs because, apparently, I didn't fit the criteria. How ironic is it that, for the first time ever, I felt upset about being blessed enough to not qualify for supplemental financial aid? Another hurdle to overcome in my long journey to wellness. I stayed positive, positive enough to trust God's plan but worried a bit about paying the hefty hospital bill that amounted to hundreds of thousands of dollars since I was being charged over $400 a day. I still kept the faith. By now, I was starting to feel internally and mentally weak as well because of all the stress about my bills and how I was going to pay.

So in other words, the only healthy thing in my body was also beginning to get tired of all the overthinking and constant stress. I was in a fix, and I didn't know what to do. I felt like I was let down by the entire world, not just society. I had served my community and country, but the community and state couldn't help me during the worst time of my life. Was my life not worth anything at all? I wanted to give up.

I wasn't working anymore, so my insurance was revoked. I felt failed by the system. I felt like I had no value or worth in the eyes of society, which I've served as a nurse. I've always helped people as much as I could. Even with so much at stake, I never thought twice before helping somebody because if God has made me capable enough to help somebody, that's an honor in itself for me. So I cherished every opportunity to help whoever I could, as much as I could. I felt blessed to have served as a nurse, to be helping people every day and providing them encouragement and words of wisdom to strengthen their faith. I felt privileged to be comforting someone else and to be offering a shoulder to cry on.

Then and there, I wanted to cry my heart out and scream out really loud to let my frustration out. How could I have comforted everyone my entire life, but I had nobody to comfort me? But instead, I turned to God, just like always. I asked him for help, and I expected his help. Whenever I ask him for anything at all, I pray with full faith of receiving whatever I'd asked for. I knew he wouldn't let me down unlike the rest of the world.

The spinal injury wasn't the main problem. The problem was the repercussions of that injury. I was paralyzed from the waist down. I felt no sensation in any part of my body from the waist down. Times kept getting tougher and tougher, and surprisingly, somehow I did too. I knew God had a plan for me. I knew this wasn't the time for me to go. I wasn't getting worse, despite no progress, and my primary goal was to focus on the positive.

The doctors suggested the end-of-life care, but there was no way I was going to accept that. The doctors told me that they'd be sending for me to discuss end-of-life care options, but I refused right away. I knew if I accepted that as my fate, it'd eventually come true. My insurance had already relapsed. I didn't know what to do, but I kept the faith. Even if I got better, I was looking at a complicated life full of trials and financial burdens.

I needed a loan from the bank, but all my requests kept getting rejected because, obviously, there was absolutely no security in loaning a terminally-ill person money. So I somehow still managed to keep the faith and look for hope and find answers from God. I was in the hospital bed since I couldn't move, and my body was practically useless in terms of functioning and movement. I started praying all the time. It was like I was talking to God.

I had nobody else at this point, so I figured, why not? I had God; it had always been that way. Every morning I opened my eyes and saw another sunrise. It was because God loved me. Every time I was capable enough to get up and go to work, it was because God loved me. Every paycheck I received was God rewarding me for my hard work, so how could I question his love for me at this moment when I should trust it the most? I would've died in the bathtub that day if that was to happen, but as I said, I survived it for a reason. The reason was that God loved me.

O Lord, heal me, for my bones are shaking with terror.
—Psalm 6:2

I was shaking with terror but also faith. I knew that nobody except God could heal me. No top doctor or specialist could make this any less stressful than it already was. Even if someone were capable of helping me, it would be a miracle sent from God.

Heal me, O Lord, and I shall be healed; save me,
and I shall be saved; for you are my praise.
—Jeremiah 17:14

Only the Lord could heal me. The more I read from the Bible, the more my faith strengthened. The more I prayed, the closer I felt closer to God. I was sure this was the revival of my body.

So the revival of my body was internally coming from within myself. It wasn't a medical breakthrough. It wasn't a clinical trial's success; it definitely wasn't therapy. It wasn't the doctors or anything else except my strength, my strength and my power to believe in God and have complete faith in him. Deep down, I kept telling myself repeatedly that God did not create me and bless me and afflict trials on me just for me to go in a mediocre way that nobody will remember a few days after. I promised myself that no matter what, I need to find the strength inside me to pass this test and overcome this fear of not being loved enough by God for him to save me.

Yes, my life is God's to take and his to give, but something in my heart kept telling me, "Not yet, Ciera. There's still time," and that one voice in the back of my head is what kept me going. I knew I was destined for greatness. I had a good life that I'm very thankful for, but I hadn't accomplished anything extraordinary yet, and that couldn't possibly mean that my life was over. I wanted to love. I wanted to live; I wanted to leave my mark and touch the hearts of the people who made a difference in my life. I just knew I had to be remembered no matter what. So I told myself to gather every bit of strength and courage inside myself and fight this.

I had to fight this for me, for God! I wanted to make him proud of me because he loved the most unlovable part of me—my present state. I had nothing. No hope, no will, no use of my body, but still, here I was—alive. There had to be a reason. It just couldn't all be for nothing. I had to gain something.

I had to get out of the hospital because I knew I couldn't let these bills keep piling up and drowning me in debt that I might not ever be able to pay back. But of course, as luck would have it, I couldn't leave until I was diagnosed and treated. And of course, it had been weeks, and no doctors were able to successfully diagnose me, so it's like I was in a prisoner in my own life. I felt so stuck.

I felt humiliated because I was of no use. I couldn't work anymore. I couldn't provide for myself or care for myself. I was stripped of every basic human right for no reason that was in my power. I didn't choose to be sick. I didn't want to be helpless. I didn't choose to be dependent like a child with an adult's brain. I had to have everything done for me, and I felt useless. It was almost like I was a baby. I had to be cleaned. I had to be fed and changed. All I had was a highly-functional brain, which I intended to make great use of by relaxing it and calming myself down and with a clear mind, figuring out a plan, to get me through all these trials and unfortunate series of events one at a time.

Days passed, and the hospital started to feel less of a prison to me. The doctors and nurses seemed to have made their place in my life. I felt as if I had friends whom I could talk to and interact with. People really underestimate the importance of human interaction. It's an essential part of a balanced life.

I felt better seeing their faces. A few of the doctors and nurses had made it a habit to visit me regularly, same time every day, not to check up on me as doctors but as friends. They all attended in a group, and I called them my healing team. They shared the same faith in me, and not only that, they shared it with the same passion, which felt like a breath of fresh air.

Dr. Nair, in particular, was very kind toward me. And I felt that his undying support is what made me feel better each day and not beat myself up over being stuck in such a bad situation. Each day they'd all gather in my room, make me laugh, and give me hope to look forward to the new and improved day to come.

He's the one who gave me hope. I felt like he was a God-sent miracle. I knew I wouldn't have been okay without his help, support, and kind words of comfort. I was now beginning to have a relatively positive perspective, and I felt like God was sending me reasons to be happy. I was glad; this was finally headed toward something I felt hopeful for. Now all there was left to do was wait for my journey to take off and slowly witness the revival of my body.

Chapter 3
A New Hope

Times kept getting harder and harder for me. It was like my faith was always present, but the hope inside me kept fluctuating. This started to worry me a bit, but I kept the faith and stayed strong. I knew I didn't have myself to blame for what happened to me; I also knew I couldn't expect myself and my mind to always stay positive. There would, obviously, come a time when I'd feel like giving up hope and giving up on myself. I'm a human being; there's only so much strength I can possess. Nobody knew the amount of stress I was under except me.

No matter how much people tried to sympathize with me or felt sorry for me, none of them knew what I was going through. The pain I was in, my mental state, nobody knew anything. I didn't want to blame them either because, of course, only I knew what I was going through, which is why I felt like now I had to come to terms with my fate. I felt as if it was finally time to accept that I was going toward death.

Again, as I said, one day was a good day, and one wasn't. Some days I would wake up with all the strength in the world, and I'd feel like I can conquer the world, and some days I just felt like I want this to be over. I want this to end even if it meant for my life to end.

One day my friends came to see me. My friends were my safe place sent from God. These were the same friends whom I refer to as my healing circle. They came to see me and always lifted my spirits with positive words of encouragement. But then again, I believe their prayers and well-wishes were genuine, even though they did not know the pain and agony that I was going through.

One day one of my friends brought her children with her to visit me. She thought it'd make me feel better. It did. More importantly, it made me realize something significant: It somehow, again, gave me the strength to fight back. I realized I wanted a family. Contrary to what most people in our society told me about women not having children after a certain age, or not being able to find love because of their "bad luck,".

I've said it a lot of times, but this time I felt that I was lonely and that I hadn't done anything extraordinary in my life. This was it. This is what I wanted: a family. Not only that, but I also wanted someone else to feel the same about me. I wanted someone to expect from me the way I long to expect from someone. I wanted someone to rely on me for love, comfort, care, and strength.

Life is beautiful. And there's a lot more to life than just finding the right career and succeeding. Life is about family. My friend made me realize that I wanted a family of my own. I wanted to give love a try despite a painful failed attempt. I was so devastated how two people could stand in front of their family and friends and, most importantly, God, and they'd either not mean what they said in those vows that had the whole church teary-eyed or that they never meant it to begin with.

It was a scary thought, obviously. But I felt as if I was ready. I felt as if I was ready to deserve the love that God meant for me to be blessed with. I remember reading the Bible later that day and coming across this verse:

> *Two are better than one because they have a good return*
> *for their labor: If either of them falls down,*
> *one can help the other up. But pity anyone who falls*
> *and has no one to help them up. Also, if two lie down together,*
> *they will keep warm. But how can one keep warm alone?*
> *—Ecclesiastes 4:9*

It got me thinking that two is better than one. Had I been married, I would've felt less lonely. I would've been surrounded by a loving husband who'd keep encouraging me to fight and keep reminding me of God's love in case I felt weak and began to forget. A husband and wife were to lift the spirits of each other, and as said in the verse, how can one keep warm alone?

I realized that day, by looking at something as simple as my friend with her children, that I wanted a family and that I wanted to fight through this because I had new motive to fight through all this pain, suffering, and misery. I wanted to get better, to be untangled from the financial stress I was in, and to get back on my feet. I wanted my life to go back to the way it was, but this time I wanted to wake up every day to a person whom I loved with all my heart and children who were symbols of that love. I wanted to be a mother and wife.

I had begun to see life in a whole new light. I suddenly found a bit of strength to fight my everyday battles. And my everyday battles weren't the same as everyone else. My everyday battles didn't consist of being yelled at by an employer or my car breaking down. My everyday battles revolved around constantly worrying about the fact that I may or may never be okay again, worrying about living to see another day, worrying about what part of my body was going to fail next. So when I say everyday battles, it meant nothing like someone would think they do.

Now that I was feeling better and a bit more hopeful again, I had to also overcome my fears once again and accept reality. I had to welcome it with open arms for me to entirely accept it. The worse thing to happen to me, apart from not being diagnosed, was the fact that my illness was a spinal cord injury. The spinal cord is to our bodies what the charging cord is to our cellphones. The phone is absolutely useless without the charging cord. In the same way, our body is useless without our spinal cord.

The spinal cord is a long, thin, tubular structure made up of nervous tissue. It functions primarily in the transmission of nerve signals from the motor cortex to the body, which makes it responsible for most functions in our body. So like I said, our body would be useless without a fully-functioning spinal cord, which means that my body was basically of no function. I was paralyzed from the waist down, which meant that I couldn't walk or move my feet or do anything on my own.

Myelin is an insulating layer or sheath that forms around the nerves, including those in the brain and spinal cord. It is made up of protein and fatty substances. This myelin sheath allows electrical impulses to transmit quickly and efficiently along with the nerve cells. If myelin is damaged, these impulses slow down, which was precisely what was happening to me. There was no transmission between my brain and my body. This is what the problem was, but nobody knew what caused it or how to fix it.

Fortunately, keeping the faith and staying strong rewarded me that day. The doctors came to visit me and told me that some of my tests had come back, and the myelin sheath was expected to go back to its original form, which meant that I would be able to regain my body functions but very slowly and gradually. He said it would take a long time, and I should not get my hopes up for immediate recovery but keep the faith because now is the time I'll be needing the most strength to fight through this, and I'll have to work harder than ever to get better.

I don't remember a lot from that day, but I remember tears streaming down my face. I remember crying my heart out with joy and thanking the Lord for all his mercy and blessings. It was a new life that was given to me. The doctors kept asking me repetitively to not get my hopes up, but I just smiled and said to myself, "You don't know, Ciera."

I'm a reasonable person. I have worked as a nurse for twenty-two years, so I am aware that my condition was still very serious, but at that moment, I didn't care enough to acknowledge any of the negative. All I kept telling myself was that I wasn't getting worse, which was just what I needed to hear to feel better. So after rejoicing for a brief moment, I started to worry about my course of action. I still didn't know what to do about the bills, which would now be twice as much since the doctors were finally on to something.

The next prognosis stated that there were very minute changes in my body, which indicated recovery. I was still in the hospital, and my next goal was to get out of the hospital. I didn't want those four walls to be familiar anymore. I wanted to feel better and heal in a better environment, not one that would constantly remind me of how sick I was.

God sent another angel in my life at that moment. My friend Lucy was who kept me going at that very moment. Her laughter raised my spirits and filled my heart with hope and joy. Lucy read the Bible out to me every day without fail. She is the reason I realized that God had finally answered my prayers and I was out of the water, the waters of misery and desperation. This realization brought a new hope within me, the hope to fight even harder and overcome everything that I had faced so that I could be an epitome of strength later on for people with the same battles as me.

I had fighting levels in my life. With strength, faith, and determination, I would overcome every trial and be one step closer to getting my life back. From almost giving up and not wanting to live anymore to being a fighter and fighting for my health, I could finally see a gleam of hope. Lucy continued to read the Bible out to me every day, and it strengthened my faith. I felt as if it brought me closer and closer to God each time.

I was thinking about getting better, and I was finally looking forward to life now. My primary focus was my health, not the money and the struggles to come. I wanted to get out of the condition I was in and look forward to my new life; I wanted to live to the fullest this time. I felt a gush of positivity and hope as I thought about my new life. My road to recovery had almost begun.

I started praying to God even more now; I needed him to bless me with strength and encouragement. The doctors told me that I had finally started to respond to treatment. He also told me that my vitals were stabilizing. Even though I did not regain any of my physical functions, and I was still paralyzed, all I wanted to do was focus on the positives.

My mechanical functions weren't great either, but I was not complaining. I had a new outlook, and I knew I never wanted to go back to ever feeling desperate and ungrateful again. This is where my healing process started. I was no longer under the stress I was before because now I knew that from here on out, it was only going to get better, and that is all the relief I needed.

The downside of not being diagnosed is that no matter what happens, nobody would know to how treat you and, more importantly, what to treat you with. Something that cures one symptom could be fatal for another system, and that is how a disaster can occur within minutes, and still, nobody would know how to stop it or treat it. I was in a similar position at one point.

The doctors could not diagnose me, so they began to rule out every possible disease based on the severe symptoms. A lot of diseases have the same symptoms, and there are a lot of diseases in the world. It wouldn't be practical if they were to test me for all of them in order to diagnose and treat me. And of course, the more days I spend in the hospital, and the more tests and scans they ran, the more bills kept piling up and added more financial strain than before. Even with all that, we had no luck. I ended up getting an infection: hysteria.

While treating me for hysteria, I was covered in ice to stabilize my body temperature for a better chance to diagnose me. I was on several antibiotics, and the acid in them caused a few side effects; one of them was inflammation. It is like misfortune just kept piling up on me; the pain kept getting worse. At one point, my blood pressure went as high as 337/110, and my blood sugar went up to 400. All these signs were telling me that my body was a mess and I had no control over it; even the doctors didn't. The doctors didn't even know what to treat or test me for; they kept doing as much as they could to keep me alive.

I had bedsores from staying in bed for months. I couldn't go anywhere or move because of the immobility. I didn't expect to be going anywhere either because I needed people to change my clothes, feed me, and bathe me. I couldn't possibly think about going out and about by myself.

I realized that I always had immense faith in God. From the moment I almost drowned in that bathtub to spending months in the hospitals, being poked and prodded like a lab rat, I always had faith. The difference this time was that I had hope, more hope than before, and for the first time in a long time, I could see the results with my own eyes. It was all there in front of me, so there was no way I couldn't believe this was reality.

I was worried about survival at that point because now that the treatment had started, there were chances that my body could reject it, or that I could be misdiagnosed, or that all of a sudden, I would just stop living because of one small mistake. I knew the life I was now living and thankful for still wasn't ideal, but not a single part of me wanted to complain at all.

I remember, just weeks ago, the doctors and nurses had all given up hope on me, but I didn't, even though the doctors and nurses never admitted out loud that there was no hope in my case. I'm a nurse, so I can read that face. I take that face several times to families when I deliver bad news that would make them break down in tears. I still didn't say anything because even though they had given up on me, I hadn't given up on me. I noticed their tireless efforts either way when they all gathered to visit me and tell me about their day and engage me in conversation.

They read the Bible to me, and all prayed for me, with me. It was a great gesture of love and care. I was very grateful to them because I am someone who believes in the power of prayer. Until this day, I believe that I am alive because of God, not the doctors. I believe that God saved me and rewarded me with a new life as a reward for keeping my faith in him stronger than ever, and I was glad that I had. I know I had nobody during the worst time of my life, but I can't imagine what it'd have been like if I didn't have God. I lived and survived the worst because God appreciated my patience.

The Lord says,

> *The Lord is not slow in keeping his promise, as some understand slowness. Instead he is patient with you, not wanting anyone to perish, but everyone to come to repentance, Peter 3:9.*
>
> *You also must be patient. Keep your hopes high, for the day of the Lord's coming is near, James 5:8.*
>
> *But as for you, be strong and do not give up, for your work will be rewarded, 2 Chronicles 15:7.*

I believe that he tested me because he wanted to make me realize what I didn't: my strength. I trusted God's plan, and he came through. He blessed me beyond measures, and living my life to the fullest and dedicating it to the greater good is how I'll reward him. I was stronger, and I was ready to conquer anything with God's blessing.

Chapter 4
Pain and Struggle

Reality is pain, and reality is a struggle. Reality was finally starting to kick in. Everything was finally getting too real. At one point, I was feeling ecstatic about finally healing and getting better, but there were days when I used to be so down in the dumps when I would realize what a long way I still had to go. I realized that despite all the positive signs my body was showing, this was still going to be a long and painful journey and that I had to endure it all by myself.

I was looking at a minimum of four to five years to regain my body functions physically. There was no telling when I'd be able to work again or even if I would ever be able to go back to work. On top of it all, I had lost my insurance. I knew I didn't have enough savings to get out of this, and neither was I capable of. I was a working, middle-class citizen.

The days kept going by, and I got the news that the hospital would be discharging me soon. I didn't know how to feel. I didn't know if I should've been happy about the fact that I'd finally be getting out of the hospital or dread the fact that I was going home alone, and I was still unstable, and worst of all, I had no money to finance myself. I couldn't even afford all the medication that was prescribed to me.

Reality was that I was going to be on my own, and I didn't have anyone at all. I didn't even have control over my body. Ever since my insurance relapsed because of losing my job, which was not in my control at all, the fact that I had no insurance was the biggest problem for me. This was one thing that I believe everyone kept forgetting: I was helpless, and nobody wanted to help me.

Once a citizen isn't working anymore, they don't qualify for the standard insurance programs, and the working class doesn't qualify for any government assistance because, apparently, they can provide for themselves with the income that they get from working. At this point, I was in a fix. I had so much on my mind; I couldn't focus on staying positive for the sake of my recovering process.

I had always considered myself to be very blessed. I had a roof over my head, a car to get me to places; I had money to put food on the table every day; and I had a respected job. As a nurse, I had seen people all my life in the hospitals, they'd be under the emotional distress of their loved one's deteriorating health, and on top of it, there would always be the financial distress of not being able to pay those bills once they got better. But there was no certainty if they'd even get better or not, which was the worst.

My heart always ached seeing those families in pain, so I know my situation wasn't a punishment; it was a test of strength. Not having any insurance made things more difficult than they needed to be, but I still didn't give up hope. I knew someone out there was going to help me. I knew that I wouldn't be left alone to rot after being a responsible citizen all my life. I believed I was entitled to receiving help, and if I tried hard enough to make them realize my situation, they'd understand someday.

I couldn't stomach the thought that I had gone from having everything to having nothing, from being blessed with the best of everything to begging for help. It was unfortunate, but all I had was God, and I believed every second that he was enough.

The day I got discharged had started to approach, and I still hadn't made any arrangements because I kept getting rejected. From one insurance program to another, I was told I didn't qualify for anything. I had to do something; the anxiety was killing me just as much as my medical condition was. I was naïve to the perception that a common working-class person could be faced with situations so traumatic and detrimental.

I couldn't work for a long time, and there was no way any bank was going to give money to someone who had no way of paying it off. I had to give up my assets, and even then, I didn't think it'd be enough. I applied for Social Security Disability; it was a program for disabled people to get financial assistance. There was a certain criterion to qualify for this program as well, and luckily, I checked all the boxes to qualify for it. I had a spinal cord injury, and I was disabled, which made me entitled to receiving aid from Social Security Disability.

By this time, the more trials I was faced with, the more I felt like somehow I kept getting stronger. To my despair, I got rejected by Social Security Disability. I didn't know what were the grounds for rejection, but I remember instead of drowning myself in self-pity, I stayed strong. Like I said, I was a good citizen. I had a good credit score, and I'd been paying for twenty-two years. But I still got rejected. I was told that in order to qualify for Social Security Disability, they'd calculate your taxes from last year. Last year I was a healthy person with a stable job, and I wasn't in need of any assistance, neither did I ever imagine in my wildest dreams that I'd ever be put into a situation this terrible.

I still didn't give up and applied again and to other government assistance programs as well. At that point, I really didn't care who accepted to help me and what programs I got rejected from. All I knew was that I had to do whatever it takes and provide for myself. I couldn't walk, I was still bedridden, but I cherished my spirit and inability to give up. I was grateful to God for keeping me sane and strong enough to keep trying despite having several reasons to quit. I knew the more I struggled, the more I'd make God proud, and he'd elevate me once this trial ends.

I was left with nothing except bills and misery. Even though I was in agony, I accepted reality painfully and knew I would find a way out of this God's plan; I was here for a reason. I was about to get discharged, and I was coming out of hospital care, with nobody by my side to help me. The hospital recommended to transfer me to a long-term care facility because I couldn't take care of myself at that moment. I got rejected by the care facility for not having insurance. It was sad to know how bad I was struggling to get somebody to care for me because I couldn't care for myself.

The hospital then had no choice but to discharge me to my house. I couldn't be alone there; I knew I could die because of how helpless I'd be. I needed two people just to turn in bed. How anybody expected me to be home and care for myself was beyond me.

I decided to call my sister, I don't know why I did since she lived in another country, but at that point, I felt like she was my only chance at being cared for. I was concerned because even though I had longed to get outside the hospital, I knew I was going out of professional care and that if anything were to happen, it could've been fatal.

I called my sister, and she agreed to come take me home from the hospital and stay with me until I got better. I didn't expect her to say no, honestly, because she's family, and no matter how busy we get in our lives, she'll always be my sister. I began to start writing letters to the embassy for my sister to get a visa. I explained to them the entire situation, about how crucial it was, because I had no other caretaker and that my condition was critical.

A social worker was assigned to us; her name was Eunice. She guided us and helped us get the visa for my sister; finally, something I could worry less about. My sister completed her travel arrangements to come to me and take me from the hospital when I got discharged. I couldn't be discharged unless and until I had a caretaker to accompany me home.

I refused to be anything but grateful. God had already blessed me with a new life; I just had to make sure I made the most out of it. I began to focus on the positives; I was finally going home, and that was progress beyond measure. Even though I still had trouble finding help financially because all the insurance companies kept rejecting me, I refused to acknowledge any hurdles. No matter how big or significant they were, the hurdles that seemed like mountains were like molehills to me.

Even though I felt as if God has blessed me with enough strength to move mountains, I didn't want to let fear take over me. I knew I was stronger because God had given me a new life. I hadn't worked for four complete months at that time; I was in the hospital all that time. I hadn't earned a single penny in four months; on the contrary, I was drowning in debt, bills, and payments more and more each day.

For most people, missing one paycheck sets them back significantly. It is a great deal to everyone. I had lost four paychecks, and I didn't know when my next paycheck was coming. I wasn't aware of how long I'd be bedridden because the longer I stayed sick and paralyzed, the longer it'd take for me to go back to work and start earning to pay all the bills and debt.

The hospital recommended a facility for physical therapy for me to be at, but again, I had no insurance, so I didn't qualify for that either. It's funny how worthless someone would think my life had become. I had to be qualifying for everything, and I still kept getting rejected repetitively. Some government assistance programs told me that in order for me to qualify for their insurance programs, I needed to have a bank balance of under $250. They didn't care enough to see the tons of bills I had and that I was disabled, unable to work and provide for myself.

Everything happened so fast; I didn't expect to be in this situation. I was just taking a bath and listening to some music, and my life changed forever. I kept telling myself that I am God's warrior, but this God's warrior was feeling helpless now, running from one place to another, trying to desperately find someone to help me and failing. Most people would've given up a long time ago, which is even what most of the people who visited me said. But I somehow got through each day with faith and strength.

I knew if God put me in this position, he had a plan to get me out of it. I didn't expect God to magically appear and hand me money and good health. But I knew and I believed that he would help me no matter what. Turns out, I was right. A few friends and my employer donated some money to help me with my hospital bills. I knew it was a great start. I felt immensely grateful. I felt worthy of life, and I hadn't felt that way in a long time. I felt blessed to be alive and breathing, but most of all, I didn't feel so alone anymore.

The hospital bill was around half a million dollars, and even if I gathered my entire life's savings, sold my house and everything else, I still wouldn't be able to pay it off. I was in desperate need of an insurance program funding me. After desperate and several attempts, calling one company to another, I was able to get a bit of financial assistance from Consolidated Omnibus Budget Reconciliation Act (COBRA) insurance.

COBRA insurance only relieved me of $157,000, which was about 40 percent of just my hospital bill. I had a million other things to worry about besides that: my physical therapy, my medication, my income, and everything else that I'd be needing now that I was a disabled person for the next few years. I still needed to take care of the rest of the bill by myself. I failed to understand why I had been paying my taxes for over two decades when in situations like these, my life isn't worth anything and the state did not care about a citizen who's been of great service to the country.

The entire problem lay in the fact that I was a working-class person who had been working for over twenty-four years. The government did not realize that I was in dire need of assistance despite several calls for help. Everyone I reached out to for help just expected me to go back to work after I'd recovered. Despite having access to my medical records and knowing the fact that I wouldn't be able to work for many years or maybe ever, nobody wanted to help.

This was a point for great realization for me. In times and situations like these, you truly learn that the world is a cruel place, and despite resisting the urge to do, every day we stray further away from God. Our everyday lives are so busy that we forget to be grateful. We forget to slow down and appreciate the little things in life. We forget to count our blessings and thank God. We forget how temporary and unpredictable life is and that we should always tell the people we love how much they mean to us.

When our lives become routine and busy, we don't care about anyone except ourselves. We only care to remember God one day a week, whereas he remembers us all the time. Every second of the day, he watches over us. He protects us and looks out for us. We keep forgetting the love that the Lord has for his people, and the worst of all, and we forget to love him back. We don't care enough to please him. We don't do any good for his people. Instead, we're selfish and ignorant.

Everything that I was going through was very unfortunate, and it broke me many times, but I am glad it happened. I am happy I got to know how much love God has for me. I am thankful to him for saving me and making me realize how worthy my life is. I was in several situations where my life wasn't worth anything, but despite all that, he still saved me. He made me realize how important I am.

> *Finally, my brethren, be strong in the Lord,*
> *and in the power of his might.*
> *—Ephesians 6:10, KJV*

Every chance we get, we should possess great strength as a gesture of gratitude. Every one of us should always take every single test and trial afflicted on us as a sign that God wants to either make or break us. It is a chance from God for even those of us who may not remember him each day. It's a sign for us to get closer to him.

I was drowning in debt, I didn't have anything, not even my own body was my own, but I still fell in love with God each day after I realized how everyone else had failed me. I had nowhere to turn to except God. I would not be worthy of being called a survivor if God didn't bless me with love, hope, and strength to overcome my worst fears. I knew I'd have to face a lot worse in the time to come, but I also knew that God would never ever let me go. And that is all I needed.

Chapter 5
Reality of Emotional Distress

I'd heard people go bankrupt after they get sick, and I finally began to understand why. I was a person who live comfortably, and this was what I went through. Nurses get paid pretty okay compared with a large percentage of the working class: the ones who work at grocery stores, food chains, in the retail industry, etc.; so I just kept imagining how terrifying it must've been for them to ever go through such an instance. Even after exhausting all my savings and collecting every small bit of money I could find, even after squeezing every single savings fund, bank account until the very last penny, I wasn't even close to even paying off 20 percent of my hospital bill. So I realized that desperate times called for desperate measures. I sold two of my vehicles. I had no idea how I was going to get to wherever I needed to be, but I knew that I had no other option.

It's like I was in a storm that never finished. But I wanted to hold on to the hope that the storm would come to pass. This was a storm that turned my life upside down. This storm left me with enormous hospital bills. On top of that, it gave me several disabilities; anxiety, depression, and helplessness above all. I was bound in a wheelchair, and my body was of no use. I had every reason to give up and believe that this storm wasn't going to pass anytime soon. But like I said, I always had hope inside of me. So something got me through this storm too, thankfully. What gave me hope was that, deep down, I knew that all this was going to pass, and that was the restoration of faith for me.

I had a long, long journey ahead of me. I told myself that I am made up of immense strength, I can withstand everything and anything that I want to, and I can endure a storm as big as this. That realization was the restoration of faith for me. Again, I say restoration of faith. That doesn't mean my faith was shaky and that it needed any restoration, but it just means that my faith somehow strengthened in my worst time and got me through such a terrifying ordeal, and for that, I am ever grateful. Because I had no bodily strength, I'm not even sure where my mind was, and I couldn't even move, but somehow, against all odds, I managed to cling on tight to my faith, and it was the best decision I ever made because it got me through everything. The times that I felt were everlasting and full of pain, that I'd never overcome the trauma and the hardships from, I did. And I couldn't ever be more grateful.

The church community was a lifesaver for me. They gathered funds for me and helped me pay for my medication. And they split the duties among themselves for the week. They even helped me subscribe to a meal service that enabled me to enjoy cooked food every day. The service was called Meals on Wheels. Even after all this time, I still get meals. They saved me from starvation.

At the same time, I still kept applying for Social Security Disability (SSD). I tried to get a hold of a private insurance company that could help because clearly, the government was not helping me.

I realized that's when I, Ciera, a health care professional, wanted to write a book on my journey. I believe that sometimes the most you can do for a person is to listen to them. There is great comfort in being listened to because it makes us feel like someone cares enough to dedicate their valuable time to listen to our misfortunes and offer comfort in return. That made me feel very positive, and if I could make someone else feel that way, it'd be a dream come true for me.

For some reason, aiding a sick person has always made me feel like my existence is validated. Perhaps that's why I chose a career in health care. It wasn't because I wanted a better life for myself, but it was because I wanted to be the reason for someone else to get a better life. And that made me feel the most accomplished I've felt in my entire life. Growing up, I'd always heard the saying, "Takers live better, but givers sleep better." This was when I decided that I was going to dedicate my life to becoming a giver and not a taker. I knew that even if I didn't have a lot financially, I'd still somehow manage to be a giver. Whether I'd be giving love or comfort or even something as simple yet efficient as encouragement and guidance, I'd always choose that over everything. And ever since, it's been a great life. I don't know if I've done enough to please God, but I can say I've always been there for his people and that alone is enough for God to bless me, I'm sure.

The Bible verses that were etched in my heart were

> *Philippians 4:6*: Do not worry about anything, but in everything by prayer and supplication with thanksgiving let your requests be made known to God. And the peace of God, which surpasses all understanding, will guard your hearts and your minds in Christ Jesus.

John 14:27: Peace I leave with you; my peace I give you. I do not give to you as the world gives. Do not let your hearts be troubled and do not be afraid.

Psalm 34:4: I sought the Lord, and he answered me, and delivered me from all my fears.

Psalm 27:1-3: The *Lord* is my light and my salvation whom shall I fear? The *Lord* is the stronghold of my life—of whom shall I be afraid? When the wicked advance against me to devour me, it is my enemies and my foes who will stumble and fall. Though an army besiege me, my heart will not fear; though war break out against me, even then I will be confident.

Joshua 1:9: Be strong and courageous; do not be frightened or dismayed, for the Lord your God is with you wherever you go.

Psalm 145:18-19: The Lord is near to all who call on him, to all who call on him in truth. He fulfills the desires of those who fear him; he hears their cry and saves them.

As the sections above delineate, we're advised to approach Jesus Christ and that he will hear us and invigorate us, trust and a beauty adequate to help us through. He will be our ever-present assistance when we're out of luck, and he can give us a harmony that passes all understanding. For me, that is amazingly reassuring.

In spite of the fact that we aren't guaranteed a simple life, we are informed that Christ will be there with us when we trust in him, that he won't give us beyond what we can deal with his assistance, and even our harsh occasions can be utilized to commend God.

Through confidence in Christ, we are given a soul of intensity, love, and discipline, and therefore, we don't have anything to fear. We can clutch his guarantees and be certain that he'll see us through even the darkest of days. Try not to worry or fear. Find your strength in him.

It very well may be so natural to surrender to stress, dread, and gloom, yet with him, we can discover quality and anticipate awesome things. He gives us trust!

One thing that jumped out at me amid posting every one of those sections, in any case, is that I never truly addressed a theme that is, by all accounts, particularly significant right now amid a twofold plunge subsidence when such a large number of individuals are experiencing serious difficulties—looking to God for quality amid harsh occasions.

Chapter 6
A Personal Reflection Thought

My sister Eunice was coming to take care of me. My body was contracted. When I came home after I was discharged, I didn't have anyone except the friends from church. They were there for me.

I needed a lot of care, I was paralyzed from the waist down, so I couldn't do anything by myself. The year before, I didn't qualify for anything, no financial assistance from the government, even though I was a taxpayer and I worked as a nurse for over twenty years, but still nothing.

I still had follow-up appointments with my doctors and physicians, and I was required to take payment because, obviously, I didn't have insurance. People had always told me that once you get sick, you become bankrupt. I didn't believe them until now. Once I went through this ordeal, I realized how right they were.

So I knew that if God had sent me in this life to be a giver, I knew that he'd give me enough strength to gather up all my debris and rise above all the pain in my life.

I know that I'm not the only one who's gone through something so bad. I've seen other people go through much worse, but it's just that there, in that moment, I didn't realize it, obviously, because my world was upside down and I had no idea about how I was going to make it through the next hour. But later I realized that it's not that bad because I am alive, and that has to mean something.

Being all by myself and constantly lost in thoughts, I started to think about one of the strongest bonds in my life: God and me. As I sat vacantly in my wheelchair or lay awake in my bed, unable to move, I realized that God had blessed me all this time beyond measure. But because I always had my legs to get to wherever I was going, and I kept going places and living that fast-paced life, I seldom had time to slow down for a moment and thank God for all that he had blessed me with.

I think this is one of the finest human errors. We pray so hard for all that we want, but we don't thank him enough. If, for a moment, we'd slow down to think about all that he's done for us and all that he continues to do despite us failing him, we'd know for a fact that even if we spent our entire lives in gratitude, we'd never be able to thank him enough for all that he has blessed us with. And so these were all my findings when I had nothing to do but lie in bed and rely on another person to look after everything I needed because I wasn't capable of taking care of myself.

I felt as though I was in captivity. Being on a wheelchair was not what I was used to. Even after seeing hundreds of wheelchairs in a day and helping people on and off them, I couldn't stomach the thought or get used to me on a wheelchair no matter how hard I tried. From pushing people in wheelchairs to being pushed in a wheelchair, I was at a loss for words.

After such a time, in your mind, it's like you're a chronic patient. I needed a change of environment. I felt as if I was in a prison, even though I was out of the hospital, and I wanted to be grateful and look forward to the next phase of healing. I didn't want to give up hope, and I never ever wanted to lose faith. Instead, I wanted to stand tall as an example for those who tend to lose faith during hard times. But the irony of it all is that nobody seemed to understand what I was going through. Yes, people get sick all the time, and yes, people do everything possible to help them, but the truth is that nobody knows how difficult what they're going through is. It's tougher for some people and easier for some. But almost everyone, sick or not, is fighting everyday battles that we don't have the slightest idea of. This is one of the biggest reasons to be kind to whoever you see because you never know what they're going through, and you never know how much your kindness can impact them.

I once read somewhere that a person was on their way to taking their own life when a stranger, who was passing by, stopped to ask for directions. The stranger behaved in such a kind way and paid attention to everything the person said that it made a great difference to the person and it made him feel special just because someone, a stranger in particular, cared enough to ask about his day. That interaction with a stranger somehow provided that person with a reason to live, and in the end, he ended up not taking his own life, instead living a great life, all because of one person who probably still doesn't know they made such a huge difference to someone's life. This is precisely why I believe it is essential that we're kind to one another.

As a strong Christian woman, I decided to move closer to my religion in order to get closer to God and establish a stronger relationship with him. I read the Bible regularly and started following my faith more than I ever had before. I am a true Christian, and I can testify that I started following the word of the book and I relied on my faith to help me emotionally overcome trauma and despair. I knew I just wanted to feel better, and I'd do whatever it took for that to happen. I knew I was God's person, and God wouldn't leave me in my time of need, he'd never let go of my hand, and he'd always give me every single shred and ounce of strength and courage I needed to make it through this.

> *I have set the Lord always before me.*
> *Because he is at my right hand, I will not be shaken.*
> —*Psalm 16:8*

I knew for a fact that God would never ever let go of me. I believe, like the verse in the Bible, that he is at my right hand and that I do not need to be shaken with fear because he will always take care of me.

> *Praise the Lord! Happy are those who fear the Lord. They are not afraid of evil tidings; their hearts are firm, secure in the Lord. Their hearts are steady, they will not be afraid.*
> —*Psalm 112:1, 7–8*

I will always praise the Lord, and I know that I'd be living a happy life because of the fear of the Lord that is instilled in my heart.

> *My grace is sufficient for you, for my power is made perfect in weakness.*
> —*2 Corinthians 12:9*

The Lord is sufficient for me. Even at my weakest, the Lord somehow reminded me that I am not weak and that he has made me up of great power, and for that, I shall be eternally grateful.

> *I know what it is to be in need, and I know what it is to have plenty. I have learned the secret of being content in any and every situation . . . . I can do everything through him who gives me strength.*
> —*Philippians 4:12–13*

I was at my worst, so I know what it is like to be in need. I was more in need than anyone else I knew because I didn't only need financial help, but I needed help to feel again, not just from my heart but from my body too. I was paralyzed, and I had absolutely nothing left in life, yet somehow the Lord filled my heart with faith and happiness. He made me look on the bright side and made me feel happy and blessed to be alive.

But the Lord is faithful, and he will strengthen and protect you from the evil one.
—2 Thessalonians 3:3

The Lord and my faith always got me through the worst of my times. I was shattered, and indeed, the Lord did strengthen me and protect me from it all.

He gives power to the weak and strength to the powerless.
—Isaiah 40:29

He gave me power when I was weak, and he gave me the strength to fight through all the trials and tests that this cruel world inflicted on me as a sole reminder that nobody is mine except him and that everything is temporary but his love is eternal.

And the God of all grace, who called you to his eternal glory in Christ, after you have suffered a little while, will himself restore you and make you strong, firm and steadfast.
—1 Peter 5:10

Finally, the Lord called me to my eternal glory, and my suffering had ended. It was the best feeling in the world, knowing that not only God sent strength my way, but he also acknowledged and rewarded me for my patience. I was strong, firm, and steadfast because that's how the Lord made me.

Times continued getting increasingly hard for me. It resembled my confidence was constantly present, yet the expectation inside me continued fluctuating. This began to stress me a piece. However, I kept the confidence and remained solid. I realized I didn't have myself to fault for what befell me; I likewise realized I couldn't anticipate that myself and my brain should consistently remain positive. There would clearly come when I'd want to surrender expectation and abandoning myself. I'm an individual; there's just so much quality I can have. No one knew the measure of pressure I was under with the exception of me.

Regardless of how much individuals attempted to feel for me or felt frustrated about me, none of them recognized what I was experiencing. The agony I was in, my psychological state, no one knew anything. I would not like to accuse them either in light of the fact that, obviously, just I recognized what I was experiencing, which is the reason I felt like now. I needed to deal with my destiny. I felt as though it was, at long last, time to acknowledge that I was going toward death.

Once more, as I stated, one day was a decent day, and one wasn't. A few days I would wake up with all the quality on the planet, and I'd feel like I can vanquish the world, and a few days, I just felt like I need this to be finished. I need this to end regardless of whether it implied for my life to end.

But just because the system and this life let me down doesn't mean that my Lord would too. In fact, I realized that no matter the number of people who keep disappearing from your life, you'd always be lucky enough to learn that God always stands beside you. He'll always love you and protect you because you are his creation, and God can do no wrong. Just knowing that God created me with so much love and time makes me fall in love with myself.

This illness was perhaps meant to make me realize just how much I loved God and that I should spend every second of my life thanking him because if, for some reason, I was stuck in such a difficult situation that tested the very best of me, I am thankful for what came with it. And that is strength in ways I didn't know existed. And I am so thankful for that because God sent me as an example for people who face hardships. I felt as if I was the epitome of strength and courage. I felt as if I could conquer the world. I know all I had to do was keep the faith, and I'd keep rising and rising!

Chapter 7
A Glimpse of Hope

What people don't understand, unfortunately, is the struggle of a woman. A woman is God's finest creation, and she is made up of immense courage and strength. Maybe that is why women have the capacity to bear so much pain and hardships in life. God knows how strong he has created them, but that certainly doesn't mean that women should be underestimated and undermined. I knew I was in a bad place, but I also knew that it'd be over soon and that God always has a plan and that, no matter what, no matter how tough things may seem right now, God is going to get you out of whatever trial you're in.

Most people don't entirely understand the severity of spinal cord injury, and as unfortunate as that is, those few included a lot of people who represent the state because they failed to provide me with assistance when I was at my worst and incapable of even moving a muscle. I was left on my own, and even though somehow it made me stronger, I can't help but think what would've been if, God forbid, I didn't have the strength to fight and, instead, have given up.

I'd always been perfectly happy on my own. Solitude was one of life's greatest blessings for me, and I prided myself in not desperately needing someone's time and affection. But I never thought that at some point in my life, I'd be contemplating whether this was a blessing or a curse because I soon found my love for solitude to turn into my fear of loneliness. And that scared me. I had been perfectly happy on my own, so why was I feeling the dire need to eliminate the silence that filled the halls? Why was I craving the touch and comfort of another person, in whatever relationship, whether it's friends, family, or a significant other?

I guess desperate times call for desperate measures. I didn't know exactly how desperate I'd be, but like I said, if there's anything that I learned, it was that I had discovered a strength within me that made me feel as if I could take on the world. That newfound strength was the courtesy of faith. And it was like the best gift I'd ever gotten from anyone, and to be blessed with a gift that great, that too from God, was the highlight of my life.

That is the main reason that I decided to write this book. Not only to give people strength during their hard times, which feel like will last forever, but also to share with everyone the gift I got from God because he was merciful and gracious to bless me with something as great. I am yet to meet someone who God hasn't been good to, whether they've gone through hard times or not. For most people, they say that their bad times feel like they'll last forever. For me, this incident was the highlight of my life, and it was exactly what I needed to believe that they really don't.

I've heard people say, "Everything will be all right in the end. If it's not all right yet, it isn't the end." And by far, that's the best thing I've ever heard because it's true! Everything really will be okay in the end, and if everything feels like it isn't okay right now, it doesn't mean that you give up hope and feel bad. It just means that there's more reason for you to look forward to something, and then pretty soon everything will be so much better than it was before. That is when you realize that you have the power to withstand the worst, so anything after that will surely be a piece of cake.

Stand in faith
Even when you can't see your way
Stand in faith
Even when you feel like you can't face another day
Stand in faith
Even when the tears want to flow from your eyes
Stand in faith
Knowing that our God will always provide
Stand in faith
Even when you feel that all hope is gone
Stand in faith
Knowing that he is always there for you to lean on
Stand in faith
Even when you feel like giving up
Stand in faith
Because he is there . . . saying, "Just look up"
Stand in faith
Even in those times you feel so all alone
Stand in faith
Hold on and be strong, for he is still on the throne
Stand in faith
Even when it's hard to believe
Stand in faith

> Knowing that he can change your situation suddenly
> Stand in faith
> Even in those times you feel it's hard to pray
> Stand in faith
> And believe that he has already made the way
> Faith is the substance of things hoped for, the evidence of things not seen
> So stand in faith
> Because you already have the victory!
>
> **—Evangelist Johnnye V. Chandler**

I was finally seeing the ray of hope in my life. It was as if the hard part was over. I was healing, and I could feel it. More importantly, the doctors saw it too! My journey of struggle was finally coming to an end. Even though it was far away, I still got a hold of the hope I had been waiting for. I felt as if my world was finally going to change for the better, and to top it all off, my newfound solid connection with God had instilled all sorts of positivity and hope in me, and for that, I couldn't be more thankful. I was also thankful for a financial rescue from National Life Group from the chronic clause that came to me just in time, but unfortunately, nothing else did. No other benefit did. And everything else was the same for all the months to follow.

For people who aren't aware of the repercussions of a spinal cord injury, it takes a long time to heal, and it confines almost all bodily functions. That is how I had felt for the past few months. My life constantly revolved around despair and hopelessness in the beginning. I felt as if I had no direction, and the struggle to wake up every day and desperately search for a sign or a reason to live was extremely testing. I felt like my life was over, and some would even say that it was. What's a life if you can't even use all your bodily functions? What's a life where you don't even know if you'll be alive the next second or not, and most critically, what's a life where an illness has taken over your entire life and you or the top-of-the-line doctors can't tell what's wrong with you and when it's going to get better or even whether or not it'll even get better to begin with?

That is how I lived each day of my life—in the uncertainty of not knowing what my life was worth anymore and if I'll ever get my old life back. For some reason, on most days, I kept recalling the day this unfortunate ordeal took place. All I could remember is waking up one morning as a normal human being and going to a well-respected job, spending the day just as I had been for the past twenty years. Unfortunately, my life had never been extraordinary. It was somewhat mundane, I'd say. I was very well-adjusted to my routine, and that's exactly how I intended for it to be.

Nothing really fascinated me to the extent that I'd obsess over it or rave about it. My relationships in life were mainly professional, and I seldom felt the need for companionship. If that doesn't describe how ordinary my life was, I don't know what will. So the day of the accident, I woke up, and I remember having an odd gut feeling for absolutely no reason at all. I remember that day felt different. I started noticing things I'd walk right past before, whether it was the crisp air, how the sun felt, how my lunch tasted that particular day, how people at work smiled at me, or just how I stood in the street and stared into nothing. I remember everything crystal clear. I don't know why, but for some reason, I do. Perhaps that day was meant to be remembered. Clearly, it has its significance even if it isn't exactly positive.

After that day, when I spent the following days and nights in the hospital, staring at the walls and not doing anything at all with all my time, I learned that life is very ordinary and unexpected. Suddenly, I had started to give more thought to the things that matter. Let's face it—it's not like my time was more valuable or needed elsewhere. The highlight of my week used to be when I'd see someone smile at me and not just out of pity. Time changed so much. I remember telling my coworkers how the highlight of my week used to be when I'd enjoy a homecooked meal prepared by myself on the weekend accompanied with a documentary.

Somehow my blissful nights that were deemed boring by others as it is turned into an even worse way to spend my nights. People were always surprised how I didn't feel the need for companionship almost all my life and how I was always so okay with being by myself. Rather, on the contrary, I preferred it. But just like every other terrible ordeal in my life, I chose to stay strong instead of believing wrong.

I always wanted to possess the amount the strength that I've somehow found today, and for that, I am so grateful. I can't say that I'm thankful for my illness or injury, but I am definitely thankful for the bond it gave me with God. I am thankful for how it strengthened my faith, and I am thankful for realizing that there is nobody in this life more reliable and giving than God is. The downside of being conquered by faith might have been my illness, but the upside of my illness was being conquered by faith. And that, despite all the struggle, makes everything worthwhile.

Chapter 8
Reviving Myself

Half a million dollars, I still owe them to this day. It's been over a year, and even though I'm better, I still haven't recovered or returned to work, but I still owe the money. This is the main reason that I felt betrayed by the system, a system that I invested so greatly in, a system that I dedicated my life to, a system that I believe I am entitled to its help but I had no luck. I fear the day when a similar instance would occur with someone who doesn't have enough strength as I was privileged to have. People give up easily, and what then? Who would the system blame then? It baffles me, honestly. It's things like these that make you truly wonder what your life is worth to others.

In today's time, it's not just people of color or a different belief from ours who are subjected to injustice. Sure, they have it worse, there's absolutely no denying their privilege, but I lose sleep over the fact that I feel the need to evaluate my worth and existence just because I feel betrayed by not getting any help from a system that was supposed to protect me even after I dedicated twenty years of hard work and service to such an unfair system.

I was not relieved in any way at all. Once you're not an earning individual in the United States, a certain type of insurance is assigned to you, the Consolidated Omnibus Budget Reconciliation Act (COBRA). COBRA was one of my greatest chances of coming out of the debt that I was drowning in and also for receiving the quality medical assistance I was entitled to. But they didn't come through either.

I had lost my insurance. I was unable to make payments ever since I got sick. I was paralyzed, and I wasn't fit or able to work no matter how hard I tried or wanted to. It was like I was stuck in a dead end with no way out. I knew I needed to revive myself no matter how bad things were looking for me. I knew that I had nobody coming to my rescue. And that wasn't a bad thing for me to say or feel. It just meant that I'd keep convincing myself that I'm stronger than I believe.

And to make everything worse, I was blindsided with an overload, an unbearable amount of bills right after losing my insurance. This was a rut for me because I didn't know what to focus on, whether I should worry about my health or the bills. If you cannot perform the tasks that a normal person does on a day-to-day basis, the government has an act of assistance for those people, and everyone who knew my condition could tell that I fit the criteria to be eligible for that insurance program. I was paralyzed and incapable of taking care of myself.

From bathing to cleaning, feeding myself, walking, standing upright, or even turning in bed, I needed help. This meant I was perfectly eligible to qualify for it under the chronic disease management clause. But unfortunately, to my despair, they didn't come through. To my bad luck, no matter how hard I tried and reached out for assistance, it didn't come through. But like I said, even though everyone thought it would break me, it didn't. In fact, it just made me feel like I have to try even harder now.

I did not get any of the benefits that I should have, but I still stood tall and went on to find comfort in knowing that I was getting better. That's all I needed for the time being. By now, I could fully be identified as an optimistic. The glass was never half empty for me. It was always half full. I took my relationship with God as the upside to the illness, I took my strength and faith as a blessing in this terrible time of my life, and I found comfort in the fact that I got through all the difficult and painful parts and that the best was yet to come. I knew I was going to get better again. There was no other way to think for me.

I could not be anything other than appreciative. God had effectively honored me with another life; I simply needed to ensure I made the most out of it. I started to concentrate on the positives; I was at last returning home, and that was advancement unimaginable. I felt like I began to forget all the bad times I had spent in pain. I felt as if all I knew was how to be strong. I knew that itself was a great gift from God. Despite the fact that I was in a financial pothole and that all the insurance agencies continued dismissing me, I would not acknowledge any obstacles.

I realized I was more grounded in light of the fact that God had given me another life. Even though I hadn't worked for a very, very long time, I still didn't feel useless and felt as if I was destined for great things. I hadn't earned a penny in four months; despite what might be expected, I was suffocating in the bills and installments which kept going up more and more every day.

> When my hopes fade
> And my dreams die.

> And I find no answer
> <u>By *asking why*</u>.
> I just keep on trusting
> And hang on to <u>*my faith*</u>.
> Because God is just
> He never makes mistakes.
> Should the storms come
> And trials I must face.
> When I find no solution
> I rest in <u>*God's grace*</u>.
> When life seems unfair
> And more than I can take.
> I look up to <u>*the Father*</u>
> He never makes mistakes.
> God sees our struggles
> And every bend in the road.
> But no mistake is ever made
> Cause he weighs every load.
>
> —Lenora McWhorter

Today, where I stand, my faith is sacred to me in a way that I cannot imagine being without it, and I would not sacrifice anything for it no matter what. If I ever questioned my existence or my purpose in life, I am guilty because I've just realized how blessed I am to be so close to God. I can't believe I'm saying this, but now that I've finally seen the bigger picture, I feel like it's safe to say that everything worked out for the better. My faith is everything to me, and I thank God for making me realizing that even if it took an incident of such great magnitude.

Statistically, I wouldn't even be alive right now because spinal cord injuries are very serious and the recovery rate isn't great. After my extensive research on spinal cord injury, I learned a lot. The more I read and understood, the more I was scared for my life and my well-being.

For the ones who don't entirely understand spinal cord injury, spinal string damage is harm to the spinal rope that causes transitory or lasting changes in its capacity. Side effects may incorporate loss of muscle capacity, sensation, or autonomic capacity in the pieces of the body served by the spinal rope underneath the degree of the damage. Damage can happen at any degree of the spinal string and can be finished damage, with an all-out loss of sensation and muscle work, or fragmented, which means some apprehensive sign can go past the harmed zone of the line. Contingent upon the area and seriousness of harm, the side effects differ, from deadness to loss of motion to incontinence. Long-haul results additionally go broadly, from full recuperation to perpetual tetraplegia (likewise called quadriplegia) or paraplegia. Entanglements can incorporate muscle decay, weight wounds, diseases, and breathing issues.

In most of cases, the harm results from physical injury; for example, auto collisions, discharges, falls, or sports wounds. However, it can likewise result from nontraumatic causes; for example, contamination, deficient blood stream, and tumors. Simply over portion of wounds influence the cervical spine, while 15 percent happen in every one of the thoracic spines, fringe between the thoracic and lumbar spine, and lumbar spine alone. Diagnosis is regularly founded on side effects and restorative imaging.

Endeavors to avert SCI incorporate individual estimates, for example, utilizing security hardware, cultural estimates, for example, wellbeing guidelines in games and traffic, and enhancements to gear.

Treatment begins with limiting further movement of the spine and keeping up sufficient blood pressure. Corticosteroids have not been seen as useful. Other intercessions differ contingent upon the area and degree of the damage, from bed rest to medical procedure. By and large, spinal rope wounds require long-haul physical and word-related treatment, particularly on the off chance that it meddles with exercises of day-by-day living.

The only thing that bothered me a lot was the fact that nobody knew what happened to me. I was diagnosed fully for days and weeks with every doctor running every possible test and scan, but the outcome was disappointing since I was charged a great amount of money without even being told that they had come to a conclusion. It was like my symptoms were being treated, not my disease, because nobody knew what had caused my disease. I had no family history of any such illness, I hadn't gone through such significant trauma, and neither had I ever gotten sick as a child. This was what kept me up on most nights, wondering, wondering what was wrong and what would happen next.

At each degree of the spinal section, spinal nerves branch off from either side of the spinal string and exit between a couple of vertebrae to innervate a particular piece of the body. The zone of skin innervated by a particular spinal nerve is known as a dermatome, and the gathering of muscles innervated by a solitary spinal nerve is known as a myotome. The piece of the spinal string that was harmed relates to the spinal nerves at that level and beneath. An individual's degree of damage is characterized as the most reduced degree of full sensation and function. Paraplegia happens when the legs are influenced by the spinal string harm (in thoracic, lumbar, or sacral wounds), and tetraplegia happens when each of the four appendages are influenced (cervical damage).

Spinal cord injury is additionally grouped by the level of hindrance. The International Standards for Neurological Classification of Spinal Cord Injury (ISNCSCI), distributed by the American Spinal Injury Association (ASIA), is generally used to record tactile and engine hindrances following spinal cord injury. It depends on neurological reactions, contact and pinprick sensations tried in every dermatome, and quality of the muscles that control key movements on the two sides of the body. Muscle quality is scored on a size of 0–5, per the table on the right, and sensation is reviewed on a size of 0–2; 0 is no sensation, 1 is adjusted or diminished sensation, and 2 is full sensation. Each side of the body is evaluated independently.

The strength to revive myself was found by me but undeniably sent from God, and for that, I cannot thank him enough.

Chapter 9
Believing in Myself

It was particularly difficult for my family, especially my sister. She broke down and almost lost consciousness when she finally flew in to see me. She could not believe or accept seeing me like this. All our lives, she'd never seen me in such a way. We were all very well taken care of, and none of us ever got sick, especially me. Seeing me with a cold or a runny nose was a rare sight. So imagine my sister's despair when she'd just flown in from a twelve-hour flight, jet-lagged, and she hadn't seen me since ages. But the first time she sees me in a long time, it's under the absolute worst of circumstances. Imagine seeing your sister all stiff and contracted, swollen and bloated. I was not anything like when she saw me last.

When she arrived, she was in shock and cried. I appeared to be physically worse than I was on regular days of recovering from my illness. I had missed her terribly.

My sister was more than happy to help me, but she had gravely underestimated the situation. She wasn't sure if she could take care of me in a proper way because people with spinal cord injuries need special care, and the procedure and protocols are very complex. My sister didn't know if she'd be able to care for me the way I needed, and I know for a fact that she was scared of the fact that I'd let her down. But for me, all I cared about was the fact that I lived to see a new day. Each day that came, I was more and more grateful. And my sister next to me was an added bonus, regardless of whether or not she knew how to care for me. It was the highlight of my month, seeing a familiar face and being around her.

I love her dearly, and the fact that I had a family member by my side made me feel happier than ever. I thank God for this opportunity too. Regardless of the circumstances, I still got something good out of it. I got to see my sister, and that felt amazing. In fact, it was the best I had felt in a long time.

I am giving a great deal of time nowadays to training and tutoring more youthful Christian laypeople and clergymen. Furthermore, I am planning to impact pioneers and religious understudies to take up the assignment of teaching others.

It is, obviously, the assignment Jesus took up in his natural service. He did, for sure, favor the majority with his open educating. However, he gave them a lot of his opportunity to put resources into the couple of his men (the twelve) whom we call his pupils. He called them to a specific period of learning under him: "Tail me, and I will make you fishers of men" (Matthew 4:19). For three and a half years, they learned under his own tutelage and care. What's more, having been taught by him, there would have been little question in their psyches what their Master was calling them to when he stated, "Make pupils all things considered" (Matthew 28:19).

Paul stuck to this same pattern in his show individual interests in more youthful partners, Timothy and Titus among them, and he energized Timothy, generally, to train the congregation's up-and-coming age of pioneers and instruct them to do likewise: "What you have gotten notification from me within the sight of numerous observers depend to loyal men, who will have the option to show others additionally" (2 Timothy 2:2).

In spite of the scriptural observer, I understand that it is so difficult to keep up a training service and to persuade individuals to choose to separate the time it requires to give oneself to educating. By teaching, I mean crafted by expressly thinking about a select number (few, relatively few) of different Christians and helping them become all the more completely dedicated supporters of Christ, who, at that point, will turn and put resources into others similarly.

It regularly feels like a difficult task because of a portion of the issues places of worship can look with training. As a matter of first importance, teaching is a service that doesn't at first yield great measurements (however, over the long haul, the outcomes can be amazing). That lone few individuals profit by such an exceptional exertion proposes, this is a wasteful utilization of time, and numerous benefactors and pioneers are not intrigued by such an, apparently, ineffective speculation. At any rate, it runs strikingly counter to our cutting-edge suspicions and senses.

Additionally, training is hard to keep up in our bustling world. We have such a significant number of chances for great open services that group out time from our timetables that could be dedicated to expressly thinking about a couple. Moreover, among different obstacles, we appear to be significantly enchanted by open showcases of ability in our big-name culture. It appears to be stupid for individuals on the

69

upwardly portable way to VIP status to jarringly hinder their calendars to put resources into a couple of individuals.

Teaching, in any case, can be the response to some dire needs in the present church. For one, measurements give proof of a pandemic of dejection among Christians. The consideration of a guide/disciple who is dedicated to the disciple can be an incredible remedy to depression. Likewise, there is, by all accounts, a plague of frailty among Christians bringing about individuals acting in silly ways that can demolish their observer, particularly when looked with testing circumstances. Such frailty could be uniquely diminished through the experience of submitted, adoring consideration and exhortation from a specific profound mother or father.

> If you are broken by life trials
> and weary from life's defeats.
> If you have been badly battered
> and have no joy or peace.
> Give God your broken pieces
> so he will mold them back in place.
> He can make them better than before
> with a touch of his sweet grace.
> If your dreams have been shattered
> after much struggle and pain.
> Even if your life seems hopeless
> God can restore you again.
> God can take broken pieces
> and he can make them whole.
> It matters not how badly broken
> God has the power to restore.
> So we are never without hope

> no matter the shape we are in.
> God can take our fragmented lives
> and put them together again.
> So if you're broken beyond measure
> and you don't know what to do.
> God specializes in broken things
> so his glory can shine through.
>
> —Lenora McWhorter

Likewise, we observe that exceptionally capable individuals are falling by the wayside through slipups at key occasions in their lives. On the off chance that solitary they had somebody to direct them! Many fine Christians are battling with tremendous issues in their own, family and expert lives. They are committing some enormous errors in their reactions to these issues. The impact of an increasingly full-grown Christian on their lives could be what causes them to understand their issues and move the correct way.

Tragically, as in any age, we keep on discovering changes over to Christ who are dynamic in chapel yet proceeding to do numerous things incongruent with Christianity (like lying, straying on the web, and being cruel to their companions) with nobody understanding that there is such an issue. A decent disciple would observe and challenge such conduct. Simultaneously, capable youthful (potential) pioneers are ascending the clerical stepping stool because of the congregation understanding their handiness. And after that, some experience a downright awful fall. There were not kidding shortcomings in their lives that brought about the fall which could have been taken care of by a disciple.

Probably the best requirement for us pioneers is to "keep a nearby watch on [ourselves]" (1 Timothy 4:16). Being a disciple helps keep one profoundly alert. We can't request that others do what we ourselves are not endeavoring to do in any event, not for long. We are pushed to maintain ourselves trim in control to be in a situation to really help those we supporter. Paul stated, "Be imitators of me," and immediately included, "as I am of Christ" (1 Corinthians 11:1).

> God's heavenly chorus
> Proclaims before us
> That Jesus Christ is Lord!
> Forever is he.
> Before history,
> All things were made by his word.
> From lowest of depths
> To highest of heights,
> And breadth of land and sea,
> The songs are sung
> Of the battle he won.
> We have the victory!
>
> —Mike Shugart

Chapter 10
Triumphant

I was seeing Dr. Nair, my doctor. He was the man handling my case, and he is the one who got me through this terrible situation with a good-enough attitude. I am so grateful to him for all his strength and support. I felt as if I had found a friend in him, luckily. After my discharge from the hospital, I was asked to follow up with my doctors every two weeks so that they could update me on my progress. But unfortunately, just like everything else in my life at the time, this didn't work out either. Regular doctor's visits meant regularly spending money. I didn't even, for a second, underestimate the importance of those doctor's visits. But I knew I had no other option.

Knowing my progress was very important to me because I needed to know whatever was happening, if it was even working or not and if all that had been for nothing; the entire pile of bills, the pain, all those days spent in chronic suffering and even now, and the inability to be able to enjoy life or even live it normally.

Having no active insurance plan meant that I'd have to pay upfront for doctor's visits and hospital follow-ups. And as luck would have it, I was scraping together all that I could to barely survive, so paying $159 for a hospital visit seemed like a luxury to me because I could not afford it. I didn't even have enough money to buy the medication that the doctors had prescribed. On top of it all, I was told how crucial physical and occupational therapy is because a lot of my healing and recovery relied on it.

But then again, it was something that was too far out of my budget. There was a lot of medical necessity shortage and negligence but not by will, but because of lack of funds and an insurance program that catered to my needs or offered enough to assist me. Physical therapy was $150 for 30 minutes without insurance, no medical or income coverage. I was denied the second time for Social Security Disability despite fitting the criteria perfectly. What more proof did they need to believe that I was disabled?

Life is measured in daily doses
Of trials and pleasures each.
Day by day grace is dispensed
To meet our immediate needs.
<u>Comfort</u> comes to the weary
We find that which we seek.
A bridge is built at the river
And power is given to the weak.
One day's load we have to bear
As we travel on life's way.
<u>Wisdom</u> is given for the occasion
And strength to equal each day.
We are never required to stagger

Under tomorrow's heavy load.
We journey one day at a time
As we travel life's rugged road.
God's mercy is new every morning
And his faithfulness is sure.
God perfects all that concerns us
And by our faith, we will endure.

—Lenora McWhorter

For many people, not being able to work and earn means they won't be able to provide for their families, but for me, I was providing for myself, and even that was falling apart. I had lost months of work and salaries. I didn't know about to what extent I'd be confined to bed in light of the fact that the more I remained wiped out and incapacitated, the more it'd take for me to return to work and begin to work to cover all the money that I owe. I didn't even know if I'd be physically be able to work the way I used to, but I was already thinking about getting two jobs and picking up extra hours at work to try and cover the bills.

As a kid, the expressions of this psalm held small significance for me. I knew nothing yet of the surging distresses of life in a fallen world. Be that as it may, presently, I think I comprehend why "It Is Well" was dearest by my father. I also have felt agony and trouble; I also have encountered enduring and misfortune. However, I have likewise tasted satisfaction amid misery. I have found, as my father, more likely than not known, that it is conceivable to feel dismal and upbeat simultaneously; or as the messenger Paul put it, to be "tragic, yet continually cheering" (2 Corinthians 6:10).

How might we experience these opposite feelings simultaneously? How might we figure out how to be "continually celebrating" amid distress? We need the intensity of the Holy Spirit, certainly. Be that as it may, scripture instructs us to develop happiness amid distress through the day-by-day propensity for searching for God's great endowments (Ecclesiastes 2:24–26). Every day our superb Father gives comfort for the present distresses and gifts for the present delights. Satisfaction in him comes each day in turn.

Envision that minute when Jesus originally plunked down on paradise's position of royalty. Having taken on our full fragile living creature and blood, lived among us, passed on conciliatorily for us, and ascended in triumph, overcoming sin and demise, he climbed to paradise, spearheading our way, as human, into the very nearness of God his Father. At that point, Jesus ventured forward, toward the position of authority, all paradise hostage with history's extraordinary crowning celebration, a service so brilliant that even the most unrestrained of natural royal celebrations can scarcely reflect it.

The vast majority of us today don't have the classes for the sort of grandeur and situation that went with crowning ceremonies in the antiquated world. We've never seen a whole kingdom tackle all its aggregate riches and expertise to put on a once-in-an-age tribute to the brilliance of its pioneer. The excess conveys the significance of the individual and his position. Imperial weddings, most likely, have their quality, yet the rising of another king to the honored position, and that serious snapshot of setting on his head the crown that flagged his capacity, is without equivalent.

But all the loftiness of history's most gaudy royal celebrations presently has been overshadowed by the grand finale to which the best of natural services was yet the faintest of shadows. The main part of Hebrews gives us a look into this royal celebration of Christ, this minute when the God-man is officially delegated Lord of all. Initially, the scene is set: "In the wake of making sanitization for sins, he took a seat at the correct hand of the Majesty on high" (Hebrews 1:3).

At that point Hebrews cites from Psalm 2, which was a song of royal celebration for the old individuals of God: "You are my Son," God says to the new Lord of Israel. "Today I have conceived you" (Hebrews 1:5). It was upon the arrival of his climb to the position of authority that the new leader of God's kin officially turned into his "child" in filling in as his official agent to his kin. The crowning ceremony was the day, as it were, that God sired the human ruler as Lord over his kin.

Next, notice "when [God] carries the firstborn into the world." What world? This isn't a reference to the manifestation yet to Jesus's arrival to paradise, following his climb. Jews 2:5 explains by referencing "the world to come, of which we are speaking." At the end of the day, "the world," in view in Hebrews 1, isn't our natural, fleeting age into which Jesus came through Bethlehem. Or maybe the world into which God brings his firstborn here is the glorious domain, what is to us "the world to come," paradise itself into which Jesus rose after his natural mission.

The setting is, for sure, the extraordinary enthronement of the King of lords. What's more, as Jesus, the successful God-man, enters paradise itself, and procedures to its decision situate, God reports, "Let everyone of God's blessed messengers venerate him" (Hebrews 1:6). Him: God and man in one terrific individual.

Initially, God had made man "a little lower than the sublime creatures" (Psalm 8:5). In any case, presently, the radiant hosts of paradise revere him, "the man Christ Jesus" (1 Timothy 2:5). So extraordinary is this man, as an authentic individual from our race, that he not just shrouds and sidesteps the race of blessed messengers. However, in doing as such, he carries his kin with him. No deliverer has emerged for fallen blessed messengers. "Without a doubt it isn't heavenly attendants that he helps, however he helps the posterity of Abraham" (Hebrews 2:16). In Christ, blessed messengers never again look down on mankind yet up. We presently experience firsthand "things into which blessed messengers long to look" (1 Peter 1:12).

This new King of the universe is, for sure, completely man and completely God and tended to in that capacity (citing Psalm 45): "Your position of royalty, O God, is for all eternity" (Hebrews 1:8). Refrain 12 (reverberating Psalm 102) rehashes the brilliance—"Your years will have no closure"—which is the climactic articulation of (and even overwhelms) saying, "Long live the Lord!" (1 Samuel 10:24; 2 Samuel 16:16; 1 Kings 1:25, 34; 2 Kings 11:12; 2 Chronicles 23:11).

At long last, the stupendous finale sounds the extraordinary prophet of Psalm 110, which has waited out of sight since the notice of Jesus plunking down in section 3. Again, the Father speaks: "Sit at my correct hand until I make your foes an ottoman for your feet" (Hebrews 1:13). For ages and hundreds of years, the individuals of God had sat tight for the day in which incredible David's more noteworthy child, his Lord, would climb to the position of royalty and hear these hallowed words from God himself. At that point, finally caught for us in the vision of Hebrews 1, the incredible cryptic dream of Psalm 110 was, at long last, satisfied.

Having completed the work his Father offered him to achieve, God's own Son (not just David's) has rose to the position of authority—not a royal position on earth but rather the honored position of paradise. The Father himself has delegated him King of all the universe. He has considered forward the imperial diadem and delegated him King of each related, each clan, each country.

We who call him King and Lord won't just accumulate one day with "there consecrated crowd" to fall at his feet, yet even now, he gives us the respect of taking an interest in paradise's continuous crowning ordinance service. We crown him with our commendations, both in everyday lives of ceaseless recognition (Hebrews 13:15) and together amid the assembly, as we accumulate week by week with our new related and clan in love (Hebrews 2:12).

The great enthronement of Christ has not finished, however proceeds. We see it now and experience it by confidence and take part with our commendations. What's more, one day soon, with all his reclaimed, we finally will participate in the everlasting melody that doesn't end and becomes just more extravagant and better forever.

Today I stand as a warrior of the Lord. I know that the times I've seen in this life, nobody else may not have; neither would I ever wish that upon my worst enemy. My journey has been difficult and painful to say the least, but it seemed easy, and I made it through because I had God leading there every step of the way. All I had to do was follow, and he took care of the rest. All he needed from me was an unshakable faith, and he took care of me. I am entirely indebted and grateful, and as a gesture of my gratitude, I vow to always pass it forward, will dedicate my life to now giving strength to other people in hopeless situations.

I will comfort them when they're let down by their respective support systems, and I will make them believe that even though it may not seem like it at that moment, God loves them, and the people in this life, all the success in the world, potential happiness and financial stability, all mean nothing compared to the joy of knowing that God has your back. I will do my part to make as many people believe that faith conquers all because I was betrayed by the system but conquered by faith!

www.ingramcontent.com/pod-product-compliance
Lightning Source LLC
LaVergne TN
LVHW011736060526
838200LV00051B/3180